Max Does It Again

Patricia Cruzan
Illustrated by Gloria Solly

Camryn
I hope you
enjoy the story
Patricia Cruzan

Note for Librarians: a cataloguing record for this book that includes Dewey Decimal Classification and US Library of Congress numbers is available from the Library and Archives of Canada. The complete cataloguing record can be obtained from their online database at:
www.collectionscanada.ca/amicus/index-e.html
ISBN 1-4120-6581-x
Printed in Victoria, BC, Canada

Printed on paper with minimum 30% recycled fiber.
Trafford's print shop runs on "green energy" from solar, wind and other environmentally-friendly power sources.

Offices in Canada, USA, Ireland and UK
This book was published *on-demand* in cooperation with Trafford Publishing. On-demand publishing is a unique process and service of making a book available for retail sale to the public taking advantage of on-demand manufacturing and Internet marketing. On-demand publishing includes promotions, retail sales, manufacturing, order fulfillment, accounting and collecting royalties on behalf of the author.

Book sales for North America and international:
Trafford Publishing, 6E–2333 Government St.,
Victoria, BC V8T 4P4 CANADA
Phone 250 383 6864 (toll-free 1 888 232 4444)
Fax 250 383 6804; email to orders@trafford.com
Book sales in Europe:
Trafford Publishing (UK) Ltd., Enterprise House, Wistaston Road Business Centre, Wistaston Road, Crewe, Cheshire CW2 7RP UNITED KINGDOM
Phone 01270 251 396 (local rate 0845 230 9601)
Facsimile 01270 254 983; orders.uk@trafford.com
Order online at:
trafford.com/05-1492

10 9 8 7 6 5 4

Acknowledgments

I wish to thank the following people:
Faye Gibbons, Jeanette Williford,
David Williford, Dr. Anne Jones,
Diane Shore, Claudia Pearson,
Chuck Cruzan, and Chris Cruzan.
I would like to thank the following
organizations and writing groups:
Fayette Writers Guild, Peachtree City Library's
Writers Circle, Georgia Writers, Fayette County
Library, Lovejoy Library, Fayette Recreation
Department,
SCBWI, SPAWN, and TRAFFORD.

To the businesses, churches, and bookstores that
support writers, I would like to say thanks.

I would like to thank the authors of books about frogs.

Also by Patricia Cruzan
Molly's Mischievous Dog
Tall Tales of the United States
Sketches of Life

- ONE -
The Problem

Max knew he should be in his room. Maybe Mom wouldn't see him if he slipped in. Max and his friends wanted to finish the football game. He reached for the football and missed it. Mom's words, spoken before he left, bounced around in his head. *Be home by five o'clock*, he remembered her saying.

"Come on, get the football!" yelled Tom.

When Max heard Tom shouting, he looked up. Max couldn't keep his mind on the game. "Mom told me to be home by five o'clock. I have homework to do," he said.

"Oh, your homework can wait. Let's finish the game," Tom said.

The football came towards Max again. When he reached for it, his black hair flopped everywhere. He saw the ball coming, but he missed the pass. Hearing Mom's voice made him lose his concentration.

"Max, it's time to come home," Mom said.

"Please let me play longer. The game's almost over," Max begged.

"You need to feed your frog. Don't you have homework?"

"Yes," Max said. "Please give me ten more minutes."

"No," Mom said. "Last night, you fell asleep before you finished your homework."

"Why do I have that dumb homework?" Max asked.

"Your teacher gives homework, so you can practice your skills. You practice football, don't you?"

"That's different; besides, I practice at school."

Max trudged into his room and walked over to his pet's home. Carefully, Max placed his green frog on his desk. "I'm calling you Bean because you're green like a bean. I wish I could play longer, but I can't. I have too much stupid homework," Max said.

Max pulled out his homework. While he worked, he let Bean walk around on his desk.

"Are you working on your homework?" Mom asked.

"Yes, Mom," Max said.

Soon, Max heard Mom's footsteps. He kept working until Mom came into his room.

"I brought you a bowl of ice cream," Mom said.

"M-m-m, that's my favorite kind," Max said.

Max scooped up the ice cream quickly. He ate all but a few melted spoonfuls. When he pushed the bowl to the back of his desk, it scared Bean. His frog leaped and landed right in the ice cream. Before Max could move his paper, Bean made frog prints on it.

"No, boy. Don't!" Max cried.

Quickly, Max grabbed Bean. He placed the frog back into his home. Max took out his blow dryer. He turned the switch on and aimed the blow dryer on his homework paper. Once Max finished drying the paper, he saw black smudge marks on it. His homework paper looked awful.

"Oh, no!" Max said. "What will I do now?"

To add to his problem, Mom's voice rang out, "I need to check your homework, Max. Are you finished yet?"

"I'm working on it," he said. "Could I feed Bean first?"

"Yes," Mom said. "Then finish your homework."

Max tried erasing the marks on his paper. Nothing he tried got the black marks out. He couldn't let Mom see them. Carefully, Max hid the homework paper under a book.

Max started out the kitchen door to feed Bean, but he stopped when Mom spoke.

"I'll check your homework after dinner. It's time to eat. Feed Bean quickly, so your food won't get cold," Mom said.

While Max stood outside, he tried to think of a solution to his problem. *There must be a way to get those stains out*, Max thought.

After Max fed Bean, he hurried to the dinner table. Max said the blessing and served his plate. While Max was eating, the phone rang. Max didn't answer it because he wanted to eat. He was glad Mom ran to answer the phone.

In a few minutes, Mom returned to the table. She said, "I'm going to eat quickly, so that I can help Grandmother. She fell and hurt her arm and foot. You two stay here and finish eating. Later, I'll let you know how she is doing."

During dinner, Max told stories about the character Strong Hand from one of his library books. "Strong Hand found a lost boy," Max said. "Other people looked for the boy, but Strong Hand rescued him." While Max retold Dad the story, his father chuckled because Max added many details. After dinner, Max helped Dad clean the kitchen. Then Max returned to his room.

When Max entered his room, his eyes rested on the messy homework paper. *Mom might not check my homework tonight*, he thought. *But what if she does?*

A new book on his bookshelf caught his attention. He stared at it and reached for it. Max tried to read, but he couldn't get the homework paper off his mind. To Max, there was little time to solve the problem. He didn't know how to get the spots out.

Max grabbed his paper again. He picked up his white paint to cover up the spots. When Dad called, Max stopped to listen.

"It's bedtime, Max," Dad said.

"Dad, please let me read the last two pages in my book," Max begged.

"Your light goes out in five minutes," Dad said.

Max put a small amount of paint on the spots. After the paint dried, the spots looked worse. Max read again, but he couldn't concentrate. He slipped out of bed to his desk. Once again, he tried to cover the spots up. Nothing he tried worked. *I have to figure out something. Mom can't see this paper,* he thought.

With a damp washcloth and a little hand soap, Max gently rubbed the paw print stains, but they remained. He rubbed harder. A small hole appeared on his paper. "Oh no!" he cried. With the tape on his desk, he covered the hole. The tape didn't help. Max held the paper in his hands until his head drooped.

- TWO -
Max's Secret

Max's alarm clock rang. Sleepily, he reached over and turned it off. He got up, so he wouldn't fall back asleep. Max stretched and yawned. He hoped Mom wouldn't want to see his homework. While Max gazed at his paper, he tried to think of another solution to the problem.

"Come to breakfast, Max," Dad called.

"I'm coming," Max replied.

Usually, Mom called everyone to breakfast. Max wondered where Mom was. Max stared at the bland cereal and apple juice. That breakfast wasn't the one Max wanted.

"Where's Mom?" Max asked.

"She's still at Grandmother's house. Finish eating, so I can take you to school," Dad said.

Max knew that he could keep the homework paper a secret for the time being. Mom might not see his paper at all. Dad didn't usually look at his assignments. But then he realized Mrs.

Scott would collect the homework papers first thing. If he could slip his paper in the stack on Mrs. Scott's desk, she wouldn't see it for a while.

After walking into the classroom quietly, Max placed his things on his desk. Carefully, he put his homework in his pocket. Then, he hung his book bag at the back of the room. He started back to his desk, but changed his mind. Since Mrs. Scott stood facing the whiteboard, he walked towards her desk. Max knew Mrs. Scott couldn't see him. With a quick motion, he slid his homework under the other papers. Someone else saw him, though.

"Why did you put your paper under the others?" Ken whispered.

"I'll tell you later," Max said.

When Max saw Mrs. Scott step out of the room, he grinned. He walked over to Ken's desk. Before Max could say a word, Mrs. Scott stepped back into the room. The stern look on her face made Max uneasy. He stepped back towards his desk.

"I'll be taking up the assignment in a few minutes," Mrs. Scott said.

Pandemonium swept through the room. Max and his classmates pushed their pencils over their papers to finish.

Once Max finished his paper, he lifted his library book from his desk. While he read, he looked up every now and then to see Mrs. Scott. She hadn't touched the homework papers yet. *Maybe she won't look at the papers until later,* he thought. Max was wrong. He saw Mrs. Scott pick up the papers.

Sweat poured down Max's back. He slumped down in his chair. Mrs. Scott would soon see his messy paper. He wiggled around in his seat, trying to think of what to say. Max felt relieved when he saw Cindy, the smartest girl in his class, walk up to Mrs. Scott. After Max saw Mrs. Scott set the papers down again, he breathed a sigh of relief.

Max decided Mrs. Scott had forgotten about the homework papers. He watched in horror when she reached for the papers. With his library book in front of him, Max thumbed through the pages. He glanced at Mrs. Scott again. Max saw her take a long look at one paper. *Maybe I can slip out to the restroom. She might forget about the paper,* Max thought. But when Max got up, Mrs. Scott called his name.

"Max, come here," she said.

Max's face turned red as an apple. Uneasily, he stepped to the teacher's desk. Max didn't want anyone to know about the paper. He hung his head when Mrs. Scott spoke.

"What happened to your paper?" she asked.

"M-m-my frog jumped on my desk into my ice cream bowl. Then he landed on my paper."

Before Mrs. Scott could speak, Derrick yelled from his front row seat, "Yuck! That paper looks terrible!"

"Ooh, that's gross!" Judy exclaimed.

"What's so bad about that?" Ken wanted to know.

"Quiet class," Mrs. Scott said. "Max, why is the paper so dirty?"

"When I-I-I tried to dry it, I didn't know my

hands were dirty. The dirt smeared onto the ice cream spots."

"You'll have to copy this paper over. Next time, keep your frog away from your homework paper. Wash your hands before you start, too."

"Yes, Mrs. Scott," Max said.

"Here's a new sheet. I want it by the end of the day. Work on it during playtime."

Mrs. Scott's last words stung. Max wanted to play football with his friends during playtime. On the way back to his desk, Max heard kids laughing. He wanted to climb in a hole. No hole was there to climb into.

Tears swelled in Max's eyes. He placed his hand over his forehead. No one must see his tears.

- THREE -
Weekly Reports

Max's class lined up for playtime without him. He stayed inside, copying his paper over. He wanted the old paper from the teacher's desk, but he knew he couldn't have it.

For the rest of the day, Max half listened to his teacher. When Mrs. Scott handed out the weekly papers, Max felt like a grasshopper was jumping inside. He couldn't be still. Max didn't want Mom to see the smudges on the homework paper.

After Max got his papers, he smiled. No messy paper was in his stack. With no grades lower than a B, he could play with his friends after school. He hoped Mrs. Scott wouldn't tell Mom about the messy paper on Conference Day.

When school ended that day, Max remembered that Dad had told him to catch the bus. He stuffed his papers inside his book bag to get ready to leave. After his bus number was called,

Max stepped into the hall. Then he stopped. He didn't have his library book, so he dashed back to get it. Afterwards, he grabbed a seat on the bus by Ken.

"I'm glad school is over today," Max told Ken.

Ken nodded and said, "Me too. Why didn't you play football at playtime? Are you okay?"

"I feel okay now. Can you keep a secret?"

"Yes. What is it?"

Max told his friend everything.

Ken tried to encourage Max. "Maybe the teacher didn't record your grade. I bet she put the paper in file thirteen," Ken said. "Are you coming over to play football today?"

"I think so. Without any low grades, Mom should let me. Here's my stop. I'll call you later."

Max got off the bus. When he opened his front door, Grandmother was sitting on the sofa. It surprised him to see the two casts she had on. "What happened, Grandmother?" Max asked.

"I fell and hit my foot and arm. They will

heal soon," Grandmother said. "How was school today?"

Max didn't want to reply, but he managed to say, "It was okay."

"Let your mom know you are home."

"Where is she?"

"I think she's in her room."

Max used long strides to get to Mom's room. He handed her his papers and waited for her comments.

"You had a great week!" Mom said.

"Could I play at Ken's house now?"

"You can play until 4:30 P.M."

Before Mom finished talking, Max dashed to his phone. Immediately, he dialed Ken's number. "Are you ready to play ball?" Max asked his friend.

"Yeah. I'll be in my yard," Ken replied.

Max took Bean out and played with him. When the two finished playing, Max left Bean on the floor of his room. Then he reached inside his closet shelf. With both hands, he grabbed his football. To make sure Bean stayed inside his bedroom, Max closed his door.

Before long, Max was in Ken's yard. "My team's going to win," Max said.

"Come on, we'll see," Ken said.

"Let's choose teams," Max said.

Once the teams took their positions, the football flew between the players. Max's team fumbled the ball several times. Later, Max made a touchdown. When the teams took a short break, Max and Ken talked about Bean.

"Did you pick a name for your frog yet?" Ken asked.

"Yes," Max said. "I named him Bean because he's green."

"I like that name. I want to see Bean next time I come over," Ken said.

"Sure."

When Max looked at his watch, he had little time left to play. He hated to leave; his team had the most touchdowns. Max kicked one last ball. Afterwards, he said, "I told Mom I'd be home in an hour. It's 4:23 P.M. I have only a few minutes left."

"Lots can happen before you leave. Let's play while we can," Ken said.

Max left Ken's house at 4:28 P.M. Thinking about his touchdown made Max's eyes sparkle.

When Max walked into the family room, he yelled, "I'm home, Mom!"

"Dinner will be ready shortly. Go clean up while I finish cooking."

Max hurried to his room. He opened his door slowly, so he wouldn't hurt Bean. Max looked around for Bean. His pet had disappeared. He searched under the furniture, but his frog was invisible. Max stopped his search when Mom called.

"Have you taken your bath, Max?" she asked.

"No," Max said. "I'll get one now."

"Hurry. I'm putting the food on the table."

Without looking, Max reached his hand in his partially opened drawer. Inside the drawer, he felt something cool and damp. Then something jumped out from one of his shirts. Before Max could stop Bean, his pet hurried across the room. When Bean stopped moving, Max caught him.

"You scared me, boy. I'm glad I found you," Max said.

Max knew his pet understood every word. While Max ran his bathwater, he talked to Bean. Before stepping into the bathwater, Max put Bean away. Max bathed hastily. After his bath, he threw his clothes on and hurried to dinner.

- FOUR -
A Call

That night, Max rushed through his homework. His homework always took too long. Max put his homework aside to read a new Strong Hand story. In it, Max's hero rushed to put out a house fire. When Max reached the best part of the story, his phone rang. He answered and said, "Hello."

"Max, will you help me with my math homework?" Ken asked.

"For a couple of minutes."

Max's friend needed lots of help, so it took a long time. Only fifteen minutes remained before Max's bedtime. He picked up his library book to read again. Max wanted to know if Strong Hand would rescue a trapped man in time. Before Max could read another word, Mom called him.

"You need to go to bed," Mom said.

When Mom turned Max's lamp off, he frowned. He had to find out what happened to

Strong Hand. After Mom was out of sight, Max got his flashlight and book. He turned to rest on his stomach. Then, he pulled the covers over his head and read with his flashlight. He read until Mom came towards his door again. When she got to his door, Max couldn't get the flashlight off fast enough. The reflection of the flashlight showed through the sheet.

"I told you that it's bedtime," Mom said in a stern voice. "Why was your flashlight on?"

"I had to find out what happened to Strong Hand," Max said.

"Go to sleep. I don't want you falling asleep in school tomorrow."

"Mom, could I please have ten more minutes?"

"Only ten minutes."

"Thanks, Mom."

Before he read again, Max tiptoed over to Bean's house. Max stared at his pet, wondering if the frog had dreams. "Good night, Bean," Max said.

Quietly, Max slid into bed. He used his lamp to read with this time. After reading on his back for a few minutes, Max's book fell on his chest. Max had fallen asleep. While he slept, Max dreamed of playing with Bean. Until Max lost Bean in the dream, they played together beside a pond. In his dream, Max's heart beat faster and faster while he chased Bean. Once Max woke up from the scary dream, he struggled to go back to sleep.

- FIVE -

A Project

The alarm rang and rang. Max could hardly get out of bed. He needed more sleep. With much effort, he packed his book bag for school. *I hope we have fun at school today. The day goes by faster when we have fun. I know I'll have fun at Ken's party this afternoon,* he thought.

Max started to dress. When Bean croaked, Max stepped over to see him. He put Bean in his hands. "I wish you could go to school with me today. Maybe one day I'll take you," Max said. Soon, Max heard Mom calling him.

"Max, it's time to leave for school."

"I'm coming. Let me get my shoes and book bag," Max said.

"Hurry up. If you're late for school, we'll have to go to bed sooner."

"I'll hurry," Max said.

Max didn't want to go to bed earlier. He liked

to read and watch TV at night. Without stopping to tie his shoes, he zoomed towards the car.

"Stop and tie your shoes," Mom said.

Max walked on. "I'll tie them in the car. I don't want to be late," Max said.

"You might trip over your shoelaces."

"I'll be careful."

Once Max arrived at school, he hung his book bag up. When he sat in his desk, the tardy bell sounded. *I'm glad I was on time,* he thought. *I won't have to go to bed earlier.*

While Max's teacher checked the attendance, Max did his morning assignments. He had trouble working; his mind was on the afternoon party. When Mrs. Scott started talking about the science project, Max perked up. He liked science. If he won a prize in the science fair, he would get extra spending money.

"I hope we have a winner from our class. Whether you win or not, do your best," Mrs. Scott said. "Use three books for research. Write a report from the notes you take. Don't forget to include a bibliography. Make a poster or chart to go along with your report."

After Mrs. Scott finished giving instructions, Max chose to do his project on frogs. He knew one library shelf had lots of amphibian books. If possible, Max would use Bean in his science project. Max couldn't wait to begin.

When the science lesson was over, Max struggled to pay attention. Finally, the last school bell of the day sounded. Max and his friends flew out the front door. They were anxious to go to the bowling alley for Ken's party. On the way, Max and his friends bragged about their bowling skills.

"How many strikes can you make?" Max asked Ken.

"I don't know, but I bet I can beat you," Ken replied.

Once Max and his friends were in front of the bowling alley, they rushed inside. After everyone paid for their games and put on their bowling shoes, balls rolled down the alley. At times, strikes and spares were made; at other times, balls landed in the gutter. Max made a gutter ball.

Derrick said, "I thought you could bowl."

"I can. Let's see how you do," Max replied.

Max crossed his fingers. He held his breath during Derrick's turn. Max saw all the pins go down after Derrick rolled the ball twice. *Oh, no! That can't be,* Max thought.

"Did you see that spare?" Derrick asked.

"I wouldn't brag if I were you," Max said.

"Let's see you make one!" Derrick yelled back.

Once Max stepped up to the line, he aimed the ball right at the pins. When he let go, every pin fell. "Hooray!" Max exclaimed. "Can you top that, Derrick?"

"I think so," Derrick said.

"Okay. Let's see you do it," Max told Derrick.

"Just be quiet," Derrick said.

Max stood behind Derrick to watch. Derrick's arm curved to the left, and the ball went into the gutter.

"Did that top my strike?" Max asked.

"You think you know it all because you made one strike. My team will win. You'll see," Derrick answered.

When the game ended, Max felt proud. His team had beaten Derrick's team. While his friends discussed the game, Max led everyone to the pizza buffet. Max and the other fellows set slices of pizza and cake on their plates. Afterwards, they enjoyed eating and talking together. When Max's plate was empty, he waved good-bye to his friends. After his mom's car arrived, Max eagerly stepped inside.

"How was the party?" Mom asked.

"I had so much fun," Max said.

"I'm glad. When we get home, finish your homework. I don't want you up late."

"I don't have much homework. I want to work on my science project, though. With Bean's help, I might win the $100 prize."

"How will Bean help you?"

"I'm going to do a project on frogs. Maybe Bean can go to school with me. If I win, I'll buy him a new home."

"You might win," Mom said.

When the car rolled to a stop, Max ran into the house. He walked over to Bean's home. After he took Bean out, the two played for a long time. "You're a great pet. I missed you today. Would you like to go to school? You'd have to be good. If you become part of my project, I might win a prize. I know you'd like a bigger home," Max said.

Max knew Bean listened. While Max kept talking, Bean rested in his master's hands. With Bean as a partner, Max thought he could win.

- SIX -
A Wish

The next day, Max walked over to see Bean. He paused to see Bean climb over the wet leaves and rocks inside the glass home. Carefully, Max set the frog on his desk. The frog made a wet spot right away. Max snatched a cloth from a cabinet to clean up the spot. "Why did you do that, Bean? I'm glad my homework papers weren't out," Max said.

When Max placed Bean on the floor, Bean walked all over Max's room. Before Max could catch Bean, his pet climbed into Max's closet, under a chair, and under the bed. Max struggled to catch Bean. Finally, Max caught Bean, stroked him, and put him away. "I'm glad I caught you before you hid again," Max said. "I'll see you this afternoon."

Once Max arrived at school, he questioned Mrs. Scott about the project. Mrs. Scott said, "I'll answer questions during science, so the whole class can hear the answers."

Max needed answers to his questions now. He wanted to work on the project before school started. Doing research at the library was fun. Later, when Mrs. Scott asked if there were any project questions, Max's hand shot up. Mrs. Scott called on him first.

"Do you want our papers in a notebook?" Max asked.

"That's a super idea," Mrs. Scott replied.

Before others could speak, Max asked, "How long should our report be? Could my frog be part of my project?"

"Your oral report should last for five to ten minutes. If your report is one of the top five chosen for the assembly, you can speak longer. Since your report is on frogs, you can bring your frog to school. One of your parents will have to take your frog home after you present your project."

"My mom will help me," Max said.

"I'll talk to her. We'll work out the details," said Mrs. Scott.

During the science period, Max listened closely to the questions and answers. *Bean might finally go to school with me,* he thought.

At the end of the school day, Max talked and laughed outside with his friends. When Mom pulled up in the car, he jumped inside. He couldn't wait to tell her about his day. "Today was great, Mom," Max said.

Max never said school was great. Usually, he waited until the last minute to finish his homework. He liked to play ball, instead of doing his schoolwork.

"Do I need to take your temperature?" Mom asked.

"No," Max said. "I'm not sick. Why do you ask?"

"You usually complain about school," Mom said.

"Today was different. We talked about science projects. If I won the prize money, I could buy

Bean a new home. I might be able to get a new football, too."

"I believe you can win."

"Will you get me a project board this week?"

"Do you want to stop on the way home?"

"You bet."

While Mom drove into the office store parking lot, Max helped Mom look for a parking space. "There's a space on the first row. We can get it," he said.

"That's a wonderful spot!" Mom exclaimed.

Once Mom parked the car, Max and Mom hustled into the store. Max bought a display board and some markers. On the way home, Max sat quietly in his seat. He took a pen from his book bag and wrote out a plan for his project.

The minute Max was home, he rushed to his room to take Bean outside. Afterwards, Bean walked around Max's bedroom while Max spent time on the project. At times, Bean climbed on Max's feet. Max continued to work on the project. It took Max an hour to sketch the life cycle stages of a frog. When Bean got tired of climbing on

Max, he wandered off to a damp, leafy area Max had fixed for him. Each time Bean returned to Max, his master gently stroked him and talked to him.

"You're going to be a star, Bean. Everyone will know there's no pet like you," Max said.

The frog's eyes shone brightly. Max knew Bean clung to every word.

"Quank, quank, quank," Bean croaked.

In the evening, Max worked on the project, and Bean walked around Max's room. Later, Max took a bath while Bean stayed on the bedroom floor. Right before bedtime, Max realized Bean needed food. Max hunted all over his bedroom for his pet. Bean was gone. Max didn't want his friend to be hungry.

When Max got tired of looking for his pet, he pulled back the bedcovers to rest for a while. At that moment, Max heard a noise. He got out of bed and looked around. The noise stopped.

Max returned to bed. When he reached for the lamp, Max heard a loud sound.

"Quank, quank, quank," Bean sang out.

Max pushed the covers back. Something flew through the air. Afterwards, Max got up to be sure his pet wasn't hurt. Even though Bean walked to Max's foot, Max checked him over for injuries. Bean appeared to be all right, so Max took Bean outside for food.

Without making noise, Max grabbed Bean and his flashlight. He tiptoed outdoors with Bean. After the two got outside, Max let Bean zap insects. When Bean finished eating, Max said, "I'm sorry I didn't get you out sooner."

- SEVEN -
Left Alone

Instead of sleeping until the last minute, Max got up. He sat at his desk, coloring his frog pictures for his project.

At first, Max didn't see his Mom step into his room. Then he looked up when she greeted him.

"Good morning, Max. Why are you up so early?"

"I wanted to work on my project."

"Do you feel okay?"

"Yes. Why do you ask?"

"You aren't usually up this early."

"I'd like to win the science fair."

"I hope you win. I'm glad you're working harder on your schoolwork. You're learning a lot about frogs. In a few minutes, I'll have breakfast ready."

Before breakfast, Max put Bean in a box beside him. It wasn't everyday that Bean joined

Max for breakfast. While the family ate together, Max laughed at the croaking noises Bean made. After Max finished eating, Mom told him to finish dressing for school. Max returned to his room and threw on his clothes.

In a few minutes, Mom asked, "Max, are you ready to leave?"

"Let me get my book bag and jacket."

"Hurry. I need to finish baking a cake when I get home. A friend is coming over today."

Without giving Bean another thought, Max started towards the door. He'd forgotten that Bean was in the kitchen.

After arriving at school, Max skipped to the library. He rushed to the animal shelves. Carefully, he pulled out three books. When Max saw Tom sitting at a table, he sat beside him. "Hi, Tom," Max said. "Are you working on your project?"

"No, I'm looking at this magazine," Tom said. "Take a look at these soccer champions of the year."

Max looked at the pictures. "That magazine

looks interesting, but I need to work on my project," Max said.

"Why are you working so hard on this project?" Tom asked. "You've never worked hard on schoolwork before."

"I want to win the science fair."

"Playing ball is more fun than working on a project."

"I like reading about frogs."

"You must."

While Tom looked at the magazine, Max read about frogs. After Max read for a few minutes, he showed Tom a picture. "Have you ever seen a frog like this before?" Max asked.

"No, I haven't. But I'm more interested in sports. You really like that stuff, don't you?"

"I sure do."

"Playing soccer and football are more fun. I'm heading back to class."

"I'll see you later."

Max continued to take notes. While he worked, he lost track of the time. When Max glanced at his watch, he had two minutes to get to class. He rushed to the front desk to check out his books. Once he had his library books and materials, he dashed down the hall.

"Slow down, Max," Mr. Collins said. "Remember, we walk in the halls."

"I'm sorry," Max said.

"You may go now but walk."

Max walked at a brisk pace to be on time. After he put his book bag away, he began his morning work.

While he worked in his classroom, Mom drove home. When Mom returned to the kitchen, she reached for the flour mixture, but stopped. Tiny flour footprints on the counter caught her eye. Suddenly, something jumped in her face. Flour flew all over the kitchen. Then Bean's eyes stared at her.

"Quank, quank, quank," Bean croaked.

"Bean, what a mess you've made!" Mom exclaimed. "I'll have to clean you up." Then she reached for Bean, but he leaped away. When Mom caught Bean, she took him to the pond. Carefully, she placed a little pond water

on Bean's back. Even though Mom was angry, nothing must happen to Max's pet. After she got the flour off Bean, she placed him in his home.

At school, Max worked on his reading assignment. During reading time, Max thought about Bean. He didn't remember whether he'd put Bean away or not. Nervously, Max looked at his watch, hoping the day would end.

On the way home from school, Max and Mom talked about the events of their day. When Mom told about her adventure with Bean, Max shook. He thought Mom might want to get rid of Bean. Parting with Bean would be terrible.

"Mom, I'm sorry Bean made a mess. I forgot to put him up," Max said.

"If you want a pet, take better care of him," Mom said.

"I'll try," Max replied.

"I didn't like cleaning up Bean's mess, but he looked funny with flour all over him," Mom said.

Max laughed. "I wish I could have seen him."

When Max and Mom got home, Max raced inside for a snack. From the kitchen, he grabbed an apple. Once he got to his room, he walked over to Bean's home. As he stood watching Bean, Mom called him.

"Be ready to leave for your piano lesson in thirty minutes."

"Okay, Mom," Max said.

For a while, Max played with Bean. Afterwards, he took Bean with him to practice the piano. Even though Max liked having Bean with him, practicing was hard. Bean kept crawling all over Max's feet. When Max finished practicing, he put Bean away. Then he left for his lesson.

At Max's piano lesson, he played the pieces he'd practiced at home. He grinned when his teacher said, "You've really improved."

"Thanks, Mrs. Moody," Max said.

"You're welcome," Mrs. Moody replied.

The lesson moved along rapidly. Max listened and watched Mrs. Moody play his new assigned pieces. He liked all but one of them. *That piece will take hours to learn,* he thought. At the end of the lesson, Max thanked his teacher. He smiled as he went outside and raced to Mom's car. Before he could get a word out to Mom, she asked him a question.

"How did your lesson go?" Mom asked.

"I did better today. I guess practicing helped," Max said.

"I'm sure it did. I'm glad you did well."

During the rest of the drive home, Max and Mom discussed Max's upcoming events. After Max got home, he put his music books away. Then he phoned Ken. The two boys made plans to play football. Once the conversation ended, Max did more research on his project. Later, he wrote his report. When it was time to meet his friends, Max put his report away. He grabbed his football from inside the closet. With his jacket on one arm and football tucked under the other arm, Max raced down the driveway. In a few seconds, he saw Ken.

When Max's friends all gathered at Ken's house, the boys chose teams.

Max's team got into one huddle, while Derrick's team got into another huddle. During the first game, Derrick's team had the most touchdowns. In the last quarter of the game, Max made two touchdowns. After the first game ended, Max said, "That was fun."

"Why didn't you come play yesterday?" Ken asked.

"I worked on my project."

"You did schoolwork instead of football?"

"Yes, I want to win the science fair," Max said.

"What does the winner get? I might work on my project more," Ken said.

"In the school fair, the first place prize is $100; the second place prize is $50."

"If you won, how would you spend the money?"

"On my frog."

"Why would you spend money on a frog?" Ken asked.

"Bean needs a larger home."

"Football equipment is more important than that frog."

"No, it isn't."

"It certainly is," Ken said.

"Let's talk about something else," Max said.

While the game continued, the boys talked less. When Max noticed how late it was, he stopped playing. "Oh, I have to go. I have one minute to get home. Mom told me to be home by seven o'clock. Good-bye," he said.

"I'll see you tomorrow," Ken said.

Max ran home. By the time he got there, he was out of breath.

"Did you have fun?" Mom asked.

"Sure," Max said. "I'll be in my room working on my project."

"That project must really be important to you."

"It is."

"It sounds like you're working hard on it."

"I am. I like to read about frogs."

"That is an interesting topic," Mom said.

"I'm trying to do my best to win."

"Don't you think all the children want to win?"

"I guess so."

The rest of the evening, Max spent time on his project. Before he turned in for the night, he talked to Bean. "I'm glad Mom took care of you today. I was afraid I'd have to get rid of you. Mom told me about the mess you made. I'll have to be more careful with you."

- EIGHT -
Max and Dad

The next day, Max left Bean by his bed to see if Mom had breakfast ready yet. Max looked in the kitchen, but Mom wasn't there. On the kitchen table, there was a note for Max to read.

Dear Max,

I'll be back shortly. I've gone to the store. There's cereal on the kitchen counter for you and orange juice in the refrigerator.

Love,

Mom

Max looked around, but he didn't see Dad. He heard water running, so he decided Dad was taking a bath. Max walked closer to Dad's bathroom.

"Dad, are you in there?" Max asked.

"I'm taking a shower. I'll be out soon."

A minute later, Dad's booming voice asked,

"How did this thing get in here? I want to see you, Max."

Max knew Dad's voice had an angry tone to it. He hurried back to Dad's bathroom door.

"Is there anything wrong, Dad?" Max asked.

"Close your eyes and open your hands. I have something for you," Dad said.

Max trusted his Dad, but he didn't like closing his eyes. He stood there, holding his hands out. A moist creature was placed in Max's hands. When Max opened his eyes, Bean's eyes met his eyes. Max knew he'd left Bean out again.

"Put your frog up. While I'm bathing, I don't like being jumped on like a lily pad," Dad said.

"I'm sorry, Dad. Bean slipped out of my room. I didn't know he was out."

"If you want a pet, keep him in your room."

Max turned to leave Dad's room. He petted Bean. "I've got to be more careful with you," Max said.

As soon as Max's stomach rumbled, he returned to the kitchen. He reached for the cereal and orange juice. Afterwards, he toasted a piece of bread. While Max ate, he looked at the kitchen clock. Only a few hours remained to finish his chores. Max ate quickly, so he could go bowling with his friends.

After breakfast, Max put Bean in his closet to clean Bean's home. The closet seemed like a safe place for Bean. Once he had Bean settled, Max closed the door. When Max finished cleaning Bean's home, he opened the closet door. Bean wasn't visible, so Max switched on the light. He searched everywhere for the frog. To find Bean, Max cleared out his closet. When he threw out his tennis shoes, his pet sailed through the air.

"Oh no, Bean. Are you okay?" Max cried.

The frog didn't move. Max picked up Bean and held the frog. Bean's eyes looked at Max. With a gentle stroke, Max petted Bean. After making sure Bean was all right, Max apologized. "I'm sorry, Bean," he said.

The thought of losing Bean twice in one day scared Max. He didn't want Bean hurt again. *I'll be more careful with you from now on*, Max thought. While Max cleaned his room, he kept watching Bean. When Max knew Bean was safe, he left his room to do other chores. After he started his last job, Mom returned.

"I'm home, Max," Mom said. "What time do you need to leave for the bowling alley?"

"I need to leave at two o'clock."

"Is your room clean?"

"Not quite, but I'm working on it."

Max's room had computer games, books, and clothes thrown everywhere. Without wasting time, Max crammed things into his drawers. In less than a minute, Max had all the covers pulled over his pillow. *I've set a world record for making my bed,* he thought.

When Max finished his chores, he worked on his project. After he'd been in his room for a while, Mom called him.

"Max, I found a book for your science report. It has information about frogs in it. Do you want to see it?" Mom asked.

"Yes, I'll look at it."

"Once you're dressed to go bowling, you can

work again on your project. I'll call you when it's time to leave."

"Thanks, Mom."

"You're welcome."

Max used Mom's book and the library books to take notes. He also drew more pictures to go along with the report. Before Max left the house, he had two pages completed in his science notebook.

- NINE -
Max and His Friends

The ride in Mom's blue car to the bowling alley didn't take long. Once Max arrived at the parking lot, he looked for his friends. After he saw Ken, John, and Brian, he ran to catch up with them.

"Hey, Ken, wait for me," Max said.

"Well, hurry up."

"How many boys are coming to bowl?" Max asked.

"We'll have enough for two teams," Ken said.

"Let's get our bowling shoes," Brian said.

"Will you be a captain, Ken?" Max asked.

"Yes, if John will be the other one," Ken replied.

"I will," John said.

When more friends arrived, Max said, "Let's begin. Ken, you choose first."

"I choose Max."

"Tom is on my team," John said.

After the boys chose teams, Max bowled first. Only four pins remained once he finished. Then John knocked all the pins down. The game continued with strikes, spares, and gutter balls. After two games, Max said, "I'm ready for some snacks."

"Me too," Ken said.

All the boys gulped down popcorn and a soft drink. Besides the snacks, Max ordered a sandwich with chips.

"Didn't you eat before you came?" Tom asked.

"I didn't have time," Max said.

During the snack time, Tom teased Max. "I think you should throw another gutter ball, Max. It really helped our team."

"Well, you knocked only two pins down on one turn," Max said.

"So what? That's better than no pins," Tom said.

"I guess your curve on the ball helps out," Max said.

"At least it knocks the pins down," Tom said.

"Come on, let's discuss our plans for next week," Ken said.

"We could go to an amusement park," Max said.

"That sounds like fun," Ken said.

The conversation continued. "How will we get there?" Max asked.

"My mom might take us in the van," Ken replied.

"I think my mom can drive some of us," Max said.

After the snack time, Max and his friends bowled for two hours. When the boys stopped bowling, Max's team had the highest score. He started teasing Tom this time.

"I'm glad you swing to the left when you bowl, Tom," Max said. "That curve helped us win."

"What about your gutter balls? You were lucky today. You and your team won't stand a chance next time," Tom said.

"Oh, yeah," Ken said.

"You might be surprised," Tom said.

The kidding continued until the parents arrived.

Once Max stepped inside his mother's car, he talked about the boys' plans for the next week. "Mom, my friends and I want to go to the amusement park next Tuesday. Could you drive some of us there?" Max asked.

"I'll drive some of you to the park. Who else will be driving?" Mom asked.

"I think Ken's mom will drive."

"I'm sure one of the parents will help."

When Max and Mom got home, Max strolled to his room to take care of his frog. Later, he worked on his project. Since Max's teacher had mentioned the project, he had spent hours on it each day.

- TEN -
A Crisis

At school the next day, Max rushed to catch up with Ken. “Mom will take some of us to the amusement park,” Max told Ken.

“My mom will drive too,” Ken said.

“We really whipped John’s team yesterday, didn’t we?”

“I’ll say we did. Tom’s gutter balls helped us.”

“They sure did. You don’t think his team will win when we play again, do you?”

“No. We could practice a few days without him.”

“Okay.”

The conversation stopped after Max and his friends sat down in their desks. Max started on the morning assignment on the board. He smiled when the teacher said, “We’re working in the library today on your science projects.”

After Max and his classmates finished the

assignment listed on the board, everyone went to the library. Library research time whizzed by for Max. He wrote ten note cards, while his classmates wrote only four or five cards. After the library time ended, Max's group had reading. During reading, Max planned ways to make his project better. After lunch, math, and social studies, Max and his classmates played soccer outside. When the last bell of the day sounded, Max walked outside. He got into Mom's car. His first words were, "Mom, will you let me play football at Ken's house today?"

"After your chores are done, you can play."

Once Max got home, he phoned Ken to arrange a time to meet. "Mom said that I can play after I finish my chores," Max said.

"Oh, it's too bad we can't play now," Ken said. "Let's meet at 5:30 P.M."

"I think I can make it by then. Let me get started."

The minute Max finished talking, he let Bean out. Max liked spending time with Bean, but he had to get his chores done. While he cleaned his room, he talked to Bean. "Today was fun," Max said. "I worked in the library on my science project. I wish you could have been there with me. Before long, I'll take you to school."

Bean croaked, "Quank, quank, quank."

Max knew Bean understood everything. People didn't believe Max when he told them about Bean, but he didn't care. When Max started out his bedroom door, he left Bean on the floor. "I'll be back in a second. You wait here," Max told Bean.

After Max returned to his bedroom, his door was ajar. He wondered why the door was open. Perhaps Mom had opened it. Max looked for Bean, but his pet was not in sight. He thought Bean might be in danger.

Without wasting time, Max shut his door. He ran to Mom. "Did you open the door to my room?" Max asked.

"No. Why do you ask?"

"I closed the door when I left. When I came back, it was open."

"Maybe you didn't close it tightly."

"I thought that I did. Bean is missing."

"He's probably hiding in your room."

Max scratched his head, trying to think of other places to look. After checking everywhere in his room, Max didn't know where else to look.

After ten minutes time, Mom asked, "Did you find Bean?"

"No."

"I'll help you look for him."

For thirty minutes, Max and Mom looked for Bean, without any success. Max tried to think of new places to look, but then he heard Bean's familiar sound.

"Quank, quank, quank," Bean croaked.

"Where are you, Bean?" Max asked.

"I think I hear him in the family room," Mom said.

"Bean," Max called out.

The croaking sound stopped and started again. Max thought Bean sounded like he was in pain.

"Qu-ank, qu-ank," Bean cried.

Max grabbed his flashlight. Mom helped Max search behind the drapes and furniture. To Max's surprise, Bean was behind the bookcase. By removing the books and sliding the bookcase out, Max got Bean out. He held Bean in his hands. Max examined Bean to be sure the frog was okay.

"Quank, quank, quank," Bean croaked.

Bean's voice sounded strong again to Max. While Max put Bean in his home, he breathed a sigh of relief that Bean was safe.

Until dinner, Max worked on his project. Then Mom called him.

"I'm coming, Mom," Max said.

After sitting down at the table, Max fixed his plate with Mom's fried potatoes, juicy burgers, and fresh salad. During the meal, Max didn't say much. He wanted to hurry and play with his friends.

Max started to leave the table.

"Is anything wrong, Max?" Mom asked.

"No. I need to hurry to meet my friends for football," Max said.

“You can take time to eat,” Mom said. “You’ll get there.”

Max cleaned his plate and left his house. He ran to be with his friends. Once he began playing football, he played until only a small pink light showed through the dark sky. When he caught the football the last time, Max called time-out. “I have to go now,” he said. “I told Mom I’d be on time.”

“Oh, no,” Ken said. “The game is not over. Our team is winning.”

“Let’s finish this game tomorrow,” Max said.

“I guess we’ll have to,” Ken said.

A short time later, Max walked into Mom’s kitchen with his football.

“How did your game go?” Mom asked.

“We just got warmed up,” Max said.

“That happens. It seems like when you’re having the most fun, you have to stop. There will be other days to play. Go get cleaned up. You can have extra time to read tonight,” Mom said.

“Great! I can’t wait to find out what Strong Hand will do this time,” Max said.

Max returned to his room and took a warm shower. After he finished dressing, he read from his library book. In the next chapter of his book, Strong Hand rescued a cat from a tree. Max thought the story was so interesting that he didn't see Mom appear in the doorway.

"Lights go out in five minutes," Mom said.

Max didn't know why Mom kept blowing a kiss his way at night. *I'll bet my friends' moms don't do that. I'm getting too big for Mom's kisses*, he thought. When Mom left, Max stepped to Bean's home. Max lifted Bean to his desk, since no homework papers were out. To Max, Bean looked content.

While Bean walked around on the desk, Max remembered that he hadn't fed Bean yet. With a flashlight and his frog in his hands, Max started outside. Quietly, Max slipped out the kitchen door to let his pet eat by the pond. Max knew he should tell Mom, but he didn't want to bother her. Even though it was late, Bean had to have food. After Max slipped back in, Mom stood at the door, waiting for him.

"You should be in bed. You'll be tired in the morning. What were you doing?" Mom asked.

"I took Bean out for insects," Max said.

"Let me know before you go outside at night."

"I didn't want to wake you up."

"Next time, feed Bean earlier. Put Bean away now and go to bed."

Max put his pet away. "Good night, Bean," he said.

After Max climbed into bed, the dim light from the moon shone through his window. His eyes closed within minutes of putting his head down.

- ELEVEN -
A Laugh

Max petted Bean, and he set his pet on the floor. "We can play later," he said. "I won't be gone long." Then, Max left Bean to wash his face in the bathroom.

When Max returned to his room, he picked Bean up again. "I bet you'd like to go to church with me." Before Bean could make his normal sound, Max heard Mom's voice.

"Breakfast is ready," she said.

"What are we having?" Max asked.

"Chipped beef, toast, and grape juice."

"That's my favorite breakfast. I'm coming right now."

Quickly, Max took Bean with him to eat breakfast. When Mom saw Bean, she let Max know that he'd have to put Bean in his room. After Max came back to the kitchen, he cleaned his plate.

Once Max left the table, he returned to his

room to dress. He put on his yellow shirt and khaki pants. Max and his parents left for church when everyone was ready.

As soon as Max got to church, he looked for his friends. When he found them, they made plans for the afternoon.

"Are you going to come over later?" Ken asked.

"I'd like to, but I need to finish my project. It's due this week," Max said.

"Come over at four o'clock. You'll have plenty of time to get your project done."

"I'll see if I get enough done."

Once all the boys sat down, Mrs. Johnson called the Sunday School class to order. The boys kept whispering until Mrs. Johnson stopped them. Max listened to Mrs. Johnson's discussion about being a good friend. When Mrs. Johnson asked about ways of being a good friend, Max spoke up.

"I help my friends with math," he said.

At the end of the class period, Max and Ken walked to the choir room. The boys practiced the anthem with their peers. Afterwards, Max and his friends sang in church. Everyone clapped at the end of the song.

Max wanted the service to end quickly, so he could work on his project. If it ended within the hour, he thought he'd have time to meet his friends for football. When the service ended, Max begged Mom and Dad to hurry home.

After the family left church and arrived home, Max rushed inside his house. He set the table for lunch without being asked, so the family could eat sooner. Max wanted to spend time on his report before his friends got together. After Max finished eating, he asked to be excused from the table.

Max hurried to his room and sat at his desk. His pencil moved along swiftly as he added to his report. After thirty minutes, he had several more paragraphs completed.

When Max took a break, he walked over to Bean's house. He lifted Bean to his lap and held him. While Max petted Bean, he decided on the picture he'd use for his notebook cover. He set

Bean down and started drawing the picture. With Bean serving as a model for his cover, Max drew quickly. Later, Max worked on the inside of his notebook. In a few minutes time, Max had several pages in his notebook finished. Afterwards, he set his pen down and closed his notebook. Max grabbed his football. It was time to meet his friends.

"Mom, you don't mind me going to Ken's house, do you?" Max asked.

"That's fine. Have fun. Be home in two hours."

"I will, Mom."

While Max played at Ken's house, Bean got bored. The frog hopped from Max's bedroom into the bathroom. Soon, the frog made his home there. Bean walked and climbed everywhere in the bathroom, since no one stopped him.

During the football game, Max fought to stay ahead of Derrick's team. Max's team led with the most points by the end of the game. When Max and his friends got tired of playing football, they pulled out Ken's board games. After Max played for a while, he said, “So long, everyone. I have to go now. I’ll see you tomorrow.”

Max ran home. The minute he walked into his room, a different sound caught his attention. He listened to see where the sound came from. It appeared to come from the bathroom. Nothing looked any different in his room, so Max went into the bathroom. An unusual sight made him chuckle. His frog sat by the basin, almost hidden from view. It wasn’t everyday Bean tried to share his bathroom. Max started laughing. In a few minutes, Mom stood in Max’s bedroom.

“What’s so funny?” Mom asked. “I heard you in the kitchen.”

Max put his finger to his lips to get Mom to be quiet. Afterwards, he motioned for Mom to come inside his bathroom.

“Mom, look in here,” Max whispered.

Max and his mom watched the frog move around the basin and tub. Seeing Bean in the bathroom made Mom laugh, too.

“How did Bean get in here?” Mom asked.

"I guess he walked in. I left him out in my room."

"He looks funny next to the basin, but remember, you promised to take better care of him."

"I'm sorry. I will try, Mom."

"Something could happen to Bean if you don't keep him put away. With your frog around, there's never a dull moment in this house."

Max had made a mistake of leaving Bean out again. He was glad Mom hadn't scolded him. When Mom left, Max and Bean played together.

"Quank, quank, quank," Bean croaked.

"Just think, you'll be the school's favorite pet," Max told Bean.

Later in the evening, Max took Bean out to eat. The frog ate and ate. After Bean finished eating, Max spent time with his pet by the pond. Then Max took Bean inside.

After Bean was put inside his home, Max pulled out his book about Strong Hand's new adventures. Throughout the evening, until it was time for Max's favorite television show, he read. Max walked into the family room at 7:25 P.M. He took the remote control and turned the television on. In the family show, Max watched a ten-year-old boy help a friend find his dog. During the show, Max's eyes kept closing and opening. Then sleep came.

Max slept soundly. He didn't hear Mom come into the family room to turn the television off. When Mom put a blanket over him, he didn't wake up.

During the night, Max awoke. He didn't know where he was. After a few minutes, he realized he'd fallen asleep in the family room. With sleep in his eyes, Max made his way to his room. Without changing clothes, he climbed into bed and pulled the covers up. He slept until morning.

The next morning, Max heard no one moving about in the house. Without making noise, Max slipped to the kitchen. He cooked oatmeal to surprise his family. Max set the orange juice, milk, sugar, and toast on the table.

Max padded down the hall to his parents' bedroom. He tapped on their door lightly. No one answered. A harder knock awoke Mom.

"Come in," Mom said.

"I have a surprise for you," Max said. "You and Dad need to get up to see it."

To help Mom get up, Max swooped up Mom's pink robe and fluffy slippers to hand her. Then, he took Dad's navy robe and slippers to him. Mom and Dad yawned. After a few minutes, Max led his parents down the hall to the kitchen. Max knew he couldn't keep his secret much longer. The aroma of cinnamon toast and oatmeal filled the air.

"What's that I smell? It smells terrific," Mom said.

"It's something you like," Max said.

"Well, what is it?" Dad asked.

Max didn't want to spoil the surprise for his parents. "You'll see," he said, as he led his parents to the table. "Now, you may look at your surprise."

"This is a special surprise. I overslept this

morning because I didn't hear the alarm," Mom said. "Thanks, Max."

"I'm glad you like it," Max said.

When everyone finished eating, Max and his family rushed to school or work. Once Max took care of his book bag at school, he started his morning work. When his teacher selected the class helpers for the week, Max smiled. Ken and Max were chosen. Max wrote the science project date on the board. Afterwards, Ken made the announcements for the morning. When Max helped the teacher, time seemed to go by faster.

Before long, Max and his classmates lined up for lunch. Max got beside Ken to talk to his friend at lunch.

During lunchtime, Max and Ken chatted back and forth. After Max finished eating, he waved his hand in the air to get the lunchroom helper's attention.

"Could I go to the library?" Max asked.

"You can go. Be back in seven minutes," the lunchroom helper said.

"Thanks," Max replied.

Max walked with a brisk pace to the library. On the inside of the library, he headed to the nonfiction section. Once Max looked through several books on animals, he checked three out.

"I've been wanting to check out these books," Max told the librarian.

"Lots of children read books on frogs. I can hardly keep them in the library," the librarian said.

After collecting the library books Max needed, he looked at his watch. With only two minutes to make it to the lunchroom, Max left. He rushed to make it on time.

"Did you get the books you wanted?" asked Ken.

"Yes, check them out," Max replied.

"Boys, zip your mouths," said Mrs. Scott. "We need to line up without the talking. Don't you want to go outside this afternoon?"

Max and his classmates walked quietly. They liked going outside each afternoon. Max put his finger to his lips. He wanted everyone to be quiet, so they could go outside.

At playtime, Max and Tom chose teams for the soccer game. Max's team fought hard to win against Tom's team. In the end, Max's team won.

"We beat, we beat! We knocked you off your feet," said Max.

"Let's see who wins the next game," said Tom.

"My team will," said Max.

When Ken started to shout back, the teacher stopped him. "It's almost time to go home. If the talking doesn't stop, we will not come out tomorrow."

Max and his classmates got quiet. They liked the afternoon games. Once the children walked inside, they put their homework in their book bags.

Max could hardly wait to tell Mom about the soccer game. When Max started to speak, Mom asked, "Did anything unusual happen today?" She didn't finish before Max started talking, too.

"Guess what?" Max asked.

"Remember, we let others finish talking before we speak."

"I'm sorry, Mom. I wanted you to know that my team won the soccer game at school today."

"That's super. What did you learn in school?"

"In math, we worked on word problems. Ugh! Science was cool, though. We planted seeds for a small garden."

"That sounds like fun."

"Our projects are due Thursday. Mine is almost finished."

"I'm pleased with your work."

When Max and Mom pulled into the driveway, the phone was ringing. Max ran inside his house to answer it. "Hello," Max said, as he struggled to catch his breath.

Ken's voice on the other end asked, "Are you ready to play?"

"I'll check with Mom," Max said.

"Sure, but hurry. I have to work on my project some more."

"Mom said that I could come over at five o'clock."

“I’ll see you then.”

After the phone call, Max took Bean out to talk and play. While Max talked to Bean, the frog’s eyes rested right on Max. When Max’s stomach growled, he put Bean on the floor. Max walked to the kitchen to grab a snack. With his snack in his hand, he returned to his room to work on his project notebook. He worked until it was time for the afternoon soccer game. Then, he picked up his soccer ball to go to Ken’s house.

- TWELVE -

Max's Friends

Max ran outside to play soccer. He waited for all of his friends to arrive. After they arrived, Max asked, "Who's going to win?"

"My team," replied Ken.

"I don't think so," Tom said.

"We'll see," Max said.

"Your team doesn't stand a chance against Tom's team," Derrick said.

Throughout the game, each team fought to stay on top. Near the end of the game, Tom's team scored two goals. Max's lower lip drooped in disgust at the end of the game. He cleared his throat and said, "We'll beat your team tomorrow. I'll see you later."

"Wait. Let's play another game," Tom said.

"I have to go," said Max.

"You're a bad sport," Derrick said.

"No, I'm not. I have to work on my project. Mom said, 'Be home at six o'clock.' "

"I guess I'd better finish mine. Maybe I'll win first prize," Ken said.

Max waved to his friends. On the way home, he remembered what Ken had said about the project. Max thought, *I've got to work harder for my project to stand out*.

Once he stepped into his room, he talked to Bean. "My team lost today. We have to win tomorrow," Max said. "Maybe you and I can win the science fair." When Max talked to Bean, he felt better. Bean was the special friend he needed at that moment. His frog always listened.

"Quank, quank, quank," croaked Bean.

Max smiled when Bean made the croaking sound. That sound showed Max that Bean would help. Max continued his conversation with Bean until the phone rang.

"Hello," Max said into the receiver.

The voice on the other end was Ken. "Is your project finished?" Ken asked.

"Most of it," said Max.

"I'm having trouble with mine. Parts of my dinosaur keep falling off. What should I do?"

"The art teacher might help you."

"But the project is due tomorrow."

"Get to school early in the morning. Mrs. Bryant gets there early."

"Thanks for your idea. You're a good friend. After we lost our game today, I didn't know whether you'd help me or not," said Ken.

"We're friends. I was sorry our team didn't win. Tomorrow our team will win."

"Do you think so?" Ken asked.

"You know we can win," Max said.

"Yes, let's stomp the other team!" Ken exclaimed.

"That's the attitude," Max said.

After the two friends parted, Max finished his whole project. Later, he read his library book and tuned other things out. He didn't hear Mom call him to dinner.

When Mom appeared at Max's door and spoke in a stern voice, Max wondered what he'd done wrong.

"Why didn't you answer?" Mom asked. "Don't you want to eat?"

"I'm sorry. I didn't hear you because I was reading."

"Come along. Your dinner is getting cold."

Around the dinner table, Max and his family shared jokes. When the meal came to a close, everyone was laughing. Max got up to leave, but Mom stopped him.

"Whose turn is it to do the dishes?" Mom asked.

"I don't know," Max replied.

"It's your turn," said Mom.

"Is it really?"

"Yes," Mom said. "I'll help you, so you can finish your project."

"It's finished, but I'd like to read."

"I'll still help. Then you'll have time to read."

"Thanks, Mom."

"What's your book about?"

"One book is about animals. I'm reading another book about Strong Hand."

"You read lots of animal books, don't you?"

"I like animals. When I get older, I might want to be an animal doctor."

"That might be a good choice. I know you like science. If you became an animal doctor, you would be a veterinarian."

After Max and Mom finished the dishes, he returned to his room. Max didn't see Bean when he opened his bedroom door. Even though Max could not see Bean, he talked to him. Max knew Bean must not be far away because he could hear Bean's croak. Max listened again. He wanted to figure out where Bean's voice came from, so he could find Bean.

"Quank, quank, quank," croaked Bean.

Max searched under the bed; Bean was not there. After looking everywhere in his room, Max went into the bathroom. He found Bean sitting beside the bathtub.

"Were you going for a swim?" Max asked.

"Quank, quank, quank," croaked Bean.

Max spent lots of time with his friend. When Max was ready to read, he placed Bean beside his bed. With his pet near and his library book, Max read for a long time.

- THIRTEEN -
Bean's Trip

Max placed Bean in a large glass jar with holes in the top. His pet would finally go to school with him today. Once Max and Bean were in Mom's car, Max held the jar tightly. The moment Max entered the school building, children crowded around him to see Bean. They even followed Max into his room. With all the attention and questions lavished on Max, his face became like a bright star.

Madison, a girl in Max's class asked, "Where did you get that frog?"

Max couldn't answer her question before Luke asked, "What's his name?"

"His name is Bean. I got him by the pond in my backyard."

Until the first bell sounded, the questions continued. Max struggled to move through the crowd. He had to put Bean away.

During the morning work period, Max kept

watching Bean. He struggled to complete his assignment. He was ready to present his project. Finally, it was Max's turn to speak.

Even though Max smiled at the beginning of the report, his hands shook. He tried to calm down by breathing deeply. He began his report by saying, "Frogs are amphibians."

While Max spoke, the children listened intently. Max held their attention by displaying his poster and his pet. At the end of his report, his face lit up like a candle because the children clapped loudly for him.

During the other children's reports, Max's ears and eyes focused on the speaker. *This is how school should be*, he thought. *It would be great to have no math problems or homework.*

When the whole class took a break, Max left to call his mom on the office phone. He didn't notice that two boys stayed behind in the room. While Max talked on the phone, the two boys in the room walked over to Bean. Quickly, the boys lifted Max's frog out from the jar. They placed Bean inside the teacher's desk.

Once Max returned to his classroom, he looked for Bean. The empty jar caught his attention. Bean had vanished. *What could have happened to Bean? I must find him before he gets hurt. I need him for my project, too,* he thought. Max kept looking until Mrs. Scott told him to sit down. With a quiver in his voice, Max said, "Mrs. Scott, Bean is missing."

"Are you sure, Max?" Mrs. Scott asked.

"Yes. Look at the empty jar."

"Ken, will you help Max look for his pet?" the teacher asked.

"Sure."

Before the teacher could say another word, everyone shouted, "We'll help!"

"Sit down and complete your work. Max has enough help," Mrs. Scott said.

Max looked sad. He didn't think he could win the fair with Bean missing. Max and Ken searched the room, while Mrs. Scott sat at her desk. Then, Max saw the teacher pull a desk drawer open. Something flew into the air.

"EEK, EEK, EEK!" Mrs. Scott screamed.

At that moment, Max's face became as a firecracker. He felt Mrs. Scott's eyes staring at him.

"Get this frog out now, Max," Mrs. Scott said. "Is this your idea of a joke?"

Poor Max. Laughter filled the classroom.

"B-b-but, I didn't put him there," Max replied.

"If you didn't, then who did?" Mrs. Scott asked.

"I don't know. When I left the room, Bean was in the jar," Max said.

While Max continued to talk, sweat dripped down the back of his shirt. Max had to get Mrs. Scott to believe him. "Please believe me. I would never put Bean in your desk," Max said.

Soon, Max felt pains in his stomach. He struggled to convince Mrs. Scott of his innocence.

"We will discuss this during playtime. It's time for reading now," Mrs. Scott said.

To Max's horror, he had to stay in during playtime again. He didn't want to miss the soccer game today. *If I can find out who played the prank on the teacher, I can go outside this afternoon,* he thought. To solve the problem, he started listening in on other conversations. When the boys went to the restroom, Max lingered behind in a stall. No one must know he was there, so he stood quietly. While Max waited, he overheard Tom and Derrick talking and laughing.

"Did you see Mrs. Scott's face when she opened her desk?" Derrick asked.

"I sure did. Putting the frog in her desk was fun," Tom said.

"I wonder what else we could do with the frog," Derrick said.

"I'll think of something," Tom said.

Max had heard the boys say they were involved in the prank. If he could tell his teacher the truth without everyone around, he could play ball, too. *Will Mrs. Scott believe me*? *Will the other boys tell the truth? Or will they try to beat me up for telling on them*? Max wondered.

Max knew he needed help with the frog situation. He couldn't talk to Ken until lunch. The morning dragged by for Max. When the class finally lined up for lunch, Max got next to Ken. The boys talked while they went through the lunch line together.

After Max set his lunch tray down, he said to Ken, "I need your help on something."

"What is it?"

"I know who let Bean out of the jar."

"Who?"

"Can you keep a secret?"

"Yes. But how did you find out?"

"I heard Tom and Derrick talking in the restroom about putting Bean in Mrs. Scott's desk," Max whispered.

"How can you be sure it was them?"

"Derrick and Tom were the only ones left in the restroom. I waited until they got out of the restroom. Then I peeped out. When I saw them open the classroom door, I stepped out."

"Are you going to tell the teacher?" Ken asked.

"I've got to tell her."

"The boys might hear you, though."

"It's the only way I can get out of trouble. The teacher thinks I put Bean in her desk drawer. I can't win if the teacher thinks I did it. I need your help."

Before Max finished talking, Mrs. Scott said, "Stop talking. We need to get water and go back to class."

"Will you help me out or not?" Max whispered.

"I guess so. Since Mrs. Scott's busy talking to the girls, let's talk to Tom and Derrick."

Max and Ken stepped beside Tom and Derrick. "I overheard you laughing in the restroom," Max said.

"What's wrong with that?" Tom asked.

"I heard you tell Derrick that you put Bean in Mrs. Scott's desk. I've been blamed for something I didn't do," Max said.

"What makes you think I really did it?" Tom asked. "The teacher won't believe you."

"We'll see," said Max.

"Mrs. Scott thinks you did it. It's our word against yours," said Tom.

"What's going on up there? You boys need to get in line," Mrs. Scott said.

Nobody answered, but they all got in line. Max decided to tell Mrs. Scott what he had heard later.

"Everyone, close your mouths and walk in a straight line to the room," the teacher said.

When the children finished their afternoon lessons, they went outside. Max stayed behind to talk to the teacher. He told her, "I-I-I know who put the frog in your desk."

"If you knew, why didn't you speak up earlier?"

"I didn't find out until we went to the restroom. I overheard Derrick and Tom talking in there."

Max had Mrs. Scott's attention. He listened to each of her questions.

"How can you be sure it was them? Did you see them when they were talking?" his teacher asked.

"When I overheard Tom and Derrick talking, I waited in a stall. I hear them talk each day, so I know the sound of their voices. Once I knew the boys couldn't see me, I left the restroom."

"I'll check into it after playtime. When everyone gets back to the room, we'll get this settled," said Mrs. Scott.

After everyone was seated in the classroom, Max walked to Mrs. Scott's desk. While Max talked to the teacher, Derrick moved nervously in his seat. “Please believe me, Mrs. Scott,” Max begged. “I didn’t put the frog in your desk. I would never do that.”

“I’ll get to the bottom of this,” the teacher said.

Before Max sat down, his mom knocked on Mrs. Scott’s classroom door.

“Come in, please,” said Mrs. Scott.

Max froze in his spot. Being in trouble with his teacher was bad enough. Surely, Mom would believe him.

“Thanks for coming to pick up Bean. Someone put the frog in my desk earlier today. Max was just telling me his side of the story.”

“I’m sorry this happened. Did you put the frog in your teacher’s desk, Max?” Mom asked.

“No. Bean was in the jar when I left the room,” said Max.

“I believe Max was in the office when this happened. I think there are two boys who know what happened,” said Mrs. Scott.

“I’ll take Bean home. He won’t cause anymore

trouble. Please let me know if I can help you with the problem. I'm sorry someone put the frog in your desk," said Max's mom.

Max hoped his teacher believed him. If she did, he could still win a prize in the science fair.

- FOURTEEN -
An Admission

Seeing Tom and Derrick called to Mrs. Scott's desk made Max happy. He hoped Mrs. Scott could get the boys to tell the truth.

"Do you boys know how the frog got out?" Mrs. Scott asked.

"No," Tom said.

Max worked on his assignment. While Max worked, he thumped his eraser over and over. *I can't lose the prize now*, he thought. *I hope the boys will tell the truth, so I'm out of trouble.* Then, Max listened to Mrs. Scott question the boys.

"That frog didn't just jump inside my desk," Mrs. Scott said. "Do either of you know who put the frog in there?"

Neither boy said anything, so Max walked to the teacher's desk. Even though Max was nervous, he had to speak up. Before Max could say anything, Derrick said, "W-w-we wanted to get kids to laugh."

Derrick paused for a minute because Tom tapped him on his back. Max watched Derrick take a deep breath. Finally, Max heard the words he'd waited to hear. "We thought it would be fun to p-p-put Bean in your drawer. I'm sorry," Derrick said.

To help Mrs. Scott understand the problem, Max said, "Derrick's right. I heard Tom and Derrick say they put the frog in your desk, Mrs. Scott."

With Derrick's admission, Max thought he could still win a prize. Max shuffled his feet around, waiting for Tom to talk. When Max got tired of waiting, he said, "Come on, Tom. I heard you and Derrick say you put the frog in Mrs. Scott's desk."

Tom didn't want to get into trouble, so he said, "You're making that up."

"No, I'm not. I stood in one of the restroom stalls, while you and Derrick were talking," Max said.

"We need to get this settled, so we can have our reading lesson," said Mrs. Scott. "Tom, do you know who put the frog in my desk?"

For a few seconds, Tom didn't say anything. Then he said, "I-I-I helped Derrick."

The teacher asked, "What did you help Derrick do?"

Tom looked down at the floor and said, "I wanted everyone to laugh. I helped Derrick put the fr-frog in your desk."

Max grinned. He could enjoy the rest of the day. At least his teacher knew he didn't put the frog in her desk. After Tom said he was sorry, Max shook hands with both boys. "Thanks for telling the truth," he said.

When Max sat down, he felt pleased. He knew he could play soccer during the next play-time. For the rest of the morning, Max and his classmates listened to the other projects. Later, during lunchtime, Max told the other children whose project he liked best. No one knew who the science fair winner would be, but Max listened to his friends' predictions.

After the class returned to their room, Max and his classmates learned about fractions. The children wanted the lesson to end, so they could see what surprise the teacher had for them. Only Max and the teacher knew what the surprise was.

Once the teacher finished the lesson, she said, "Max, bring out the surprise now."

When Max brought out a sheet cake, the children shouted, "Look at that!" Max could barely get the cake on the table before everyone crowded around.

"I want a big piece," said Derrick.

After the children settled down, Mrs. Scott said, "I'll divide the cake into twenty-four pieces. The cake is one whole piece now. When I cut the cake, what fraction can I write, Max?"

Max came to the board and wrote $^{24}/_{24}$.

"That's right, Max," replied Mrs. Scott. "Let's enjoy our snack. When everyone finishes your slice, clean around your desks. You'll need to pack your book bags to go home, also."

Once the final bell sounded, Max slid into

Mom's car. He couldn't wait for Mom to ask about his day.

"How did you do on your project?" Mom asked.

"I did okay. I got scared when Bean was gone."

"Has the winner for the science fair been announced?"

"No, not yet," Max said.

"Who put Bean into Mrs. Scott's desk?"

"Tom and Derrick. They did it to make the class laugh."

"I'm glad you didn't put the frog in your teacher's desk," Mom said.

"I wouldn't do that."

"Who do you think will win the fair?"

"I don't know," Max said. "Do you think I still have a chance after this happened?"

"I would say so," Max's mom said.

Once Max got home, he went to his room. When he opened his bedroom door, he heard, "Quank, quank, quank."

Max lifted Bean out of his home. "How did you like school, Bean?" Max asked his pet.

"Quank, quank, quank," Bean croaked.

Max held Bean in his hands. The frog and boy enjoyed being together. Until Max made a phone call to Ken, Bean and Max played. "Can you play soccer now?" Max asked Ken.

"I'll check. Hold on," said Ken. After Ken returned to the phone, he said, "I'll meet you in fifteen minutes."

"Okay."

Max did his chores quickly, so he could meet Ken. Before he left, Max reached for his soccer ball. The ball bounced on the floor before he caught it. By holding the ball tightly, he kept it from bouncing again.

Once Max got on the field, all the boys took their positions. Neither team made a goal at first. After the boys played for five minutes, Max passed the ball to Ken. Before long, Ken made a goal.

"Your team won't make another goal," Derrick said.

"Oh, no. Just watch us!' Max shouted.

In a few seconds, Max passed the ball to John. Their team scored when John kicked the ball into the goal.

"You think you're so smart. Just wait, we'll stop you," Tom said.

"I don't think you can," Max said.

"I wouldn't brag," Derrick said.

After playing for another thirty minutes, Derrick's team caught up to Max's team. Then, Tom made another goal for Derrick's team. The boys kept playing until Ken had to go inside. At the end of the game, Max's team was behind. Even though Max was disappointed, he yelled, "We'll beat the socks off your team tomorrow! Just wait and see."

"I don't think you can," Tom said.

"Well, we've beaten your team before," Max said. When he finished talking to Tom, he walked home. Later, at home, Max tried to figure out what Mom was cooking. "What's for dinner? I'm starving," Max said.

"We're having hamburgers, salad, and fries.

Playing ball makes you hungry. I know you like hamburgers," Mom said.

"Are the hamburgers ready?"

"By the time your hands are washed, the burgers should be ready."

While Max ate, he heard Bean croaking. Max hurried to finish, so he could feed Bean. "I'm on my way!" he yelled to Bean.

The minute Max got Bean outside, his pet zapped several insects. Max let Bean wander around the trees for a while. Afterwards, Max took him inside. The rest of the evening, Max read and daydreamed about the science fair prize. When his eyes couldn't stay open any longer, he slept. In his dreams, he kept trying to find Bean.

- FIFTEEN -
The Winner

Max woke up, shaking from a scary dream. In his dream Bean had disappeared. The frog was nowhere to be seen. When Max climbed out of bed to check on Bean, his pet stared back at him. Sleepily, Max crawled back to bed. In a short time, the alarm clock sounded; Max rubbed his eyes. He turned over for more sleep, but then he remembered why he needed to get up early. He wanted to find out who the finalists were in the science fair. If he became one of the finalists, he might end up in the state competition.

Max hastily threw on his clothes. Before he left his room, he heard Mom call.

"Max, are you up?" Mom asked.

"Yes, Mom," Max replied.

"Breakfast is ready."

"Something smells good."

"What do think we are having?"

"Pancakes," Max said.

"How did you know?"

"I could smell them."

"I can't fool you. I fixed them for you and Dad because I know how much you like them."

"I can't wait to eat them," Max said.

Max put several pancakes on his plate. While Max ate, he had little to say. When the meal ended, no pancakes remained on his plate.

After breakfast, Max gathered his things for school. "Mom, could we leave now?" he asked.

"Why do you want to leave so early?"

"I think the teachers might post names of the children still in the competition. I hope my name is on the list."

"Give me a minute. I need to comb my hair and grab my keys," said Mom.

When Max opened the front door to go outside, he cried, "Oh, no! It's raining. I wanted to hurry and get to school."

"You'll see the list soon. Be patient," Mom said.

Max had trouble being patient. The rain slowed the traffic down, so he knew it would take longer to get to school. Max watched the rain pelt down on the car. “Mom, do you think the rain will stop by this afternoon?” he asked.

“I think the rain will continue throughout the day. Why are you interested in the forecast?” Mom asked.

“Everyone wants to play outside today. Later, we want to get pizza.”

“That sounds like fun.”

“I hope it stops raining.”

“You can have fun inside. Ken has some board games, doesn’t he?”

“Yes. But we like to play soccer and football.”

“It might stop raining by this afternoon.”

“I hope so,” Max said.

For the rest of the trip to school, Max thought about the afternoon activities.

By the time his mom’s car pulled into the school parking lot, rainwater covered the streets and sidewalks. When Max stepped out of the car, sheets of rain poured from his raincoat. He darted into the school building. Before he took care of his book bag and raincoat, he checked for a list of science fair finalists. No names were listed yet. Max looked around for Ken. His friend had not arrived, so Max hung his raincoat up. Before he put his book bag away, he took his favorite pencil out, along with his paper.

Max read the directions for the first assignment before he began writing. After he set his paper on his desk, his pencil flowed easily over his paper. He had no trouble writing about why he should win the science fair. He wrote for a few minutes. Then, he stopped to check his paper over for mistakes.

Before Max passed his paper in, he listened to the principal's television announcements. The children's chatter made it almost impossible to hear his name called. Quickly, he grabbed his poster and notebook. He asked Brian to help carry the poster and notebook, so he could get Bean.

Max set up his science materials on the stage, while his class filed into the assembly. When Max sat in his chair, he chewed his fingernails. Max sat there until the principal called on him to present his project. After he stepped on the stage, his mind went blank. Mom had warned him that this could happen. Max remembered what she had told him to do, so he took a couple of deep breaths. He used his note cards to help him begin his speech.

During Max's report in the assembly, he explained the life cycle drawings of the frog. He also showed Bean to the children. When he finished, he sat down quietly. Max knew he had done his best on the report.

Max watched Ann go on stage next. He listened to every word that Ann said. Once Ann finished, Max did not think that he had a chance of winning. He could tell from the children's applause that they liked her report.

After Ann sat down, Max listened to John's presentation on bees. Max knew that John's project was outstanding, too. To Max, all the presentations seemed to be going well. Max was worried about winning.

When Ken stepped up to give his project, Max smiled. Max could tell that Ken was nervous. His friend lost the place and stumbled over some of the words. After Ken left the stage, Max knew the children applauded more for Ann than for Ken. When Ken sat down, Max felt sorry for him. His friend's project was not as good as the other projects. Max hoped his friend would win a prize.

During the next two projects, Max squirmed in his seat. He couldn't figure out who the winner would be. Waiting was hard. When the last report was over, Max saw the principal stand up again. For a few seconds, Max started daydreaming. He almost missed the principal's words.

"John Williams, please step forward. You are our third place winner. Congratulations on your hard work."

Max wanted a check and a trophy like John had received. He knew John's project would be in the state fair. Max moved his legs back and forth, waiting for the results. Max tried to remember that there would be other contests; besides, he liked having Bean at school. After

Max heard Ann's name called, he placed his hand on his forehead and looked down. His eyes clouded over with tears. With a quick sweep of his hand, he wiped the tears from his eyes. He slumped down in his chair. Then suddenly, all eyes rested on Max.

The principal said, "Our first prize goes to Max Davis for the most outstanding project. His project shows detailed research and artwork. I'd like for Max and his mother to come forward."

For a few seconds Max didn't move. He sat stunned. When all eyes kept staring at Max, and Ken kept tapping him, Max knew his dream was real. With his eyes sparkling, Max walked onstage. Proudly, he took the trophy and check from the principal's hand. "Thank you," Max said.

"I wish all of our winners success at the state competition," said the principal.

For the next few days, Max walked around like his mind was in a cloud. After a couple of days, he worked on his project for the state competition. Max knew he'd done his best.

Finally, the day arrived for Max to find out the results of the state fair. When Max moved into the exhibit hall, he stared in disbelief at the red ribbon on his project. Max's eyes danced with delight. While Max stood in front of his project, he discovered a note attached to the ribbon. Max reached for it. Inside the note was a $300.00 check. Eagerly, Max opened the envelope and read the letter.

Dear Max,

Your project shows lots of hard work and effort.

Thanks for a job well done.

I hope you will submit your work again next year.

Perhaps one day, you will become a scientist. We wish you much success in the future.

Best wishes,

Mark Jones

Brittany Green

Martha Thomas

Max knew Bean would get a new home now. He had money left to buy other items, also. Later that day, Max asked his mom, "Do you have time to take me to the store? I want to get a new home for Bean."

"I will make time today. One more errand shouldn't take too long. I am so proud of you for winning the science competition."

"Could you take me to the bank, too?"

"Yes. What are you going to do with all the money you have?"

"I will put some money into savings. Bean might need something later on."

"You could put some of your money in a piggy bank at home."

"I want my own account, like you and Dad."

"I'll help you get an account. I'm glad you are saving some money."

While Max and Mom ran their errands, Max put ideas in his memory bank for future projects. When he returned home, he grabbed his soccer ball to join his friends.

Once Max got to the field, Ken said, "Congratulations on winning the state fair."

"Did you really win?" Derrick asked.

"Yes. I got a check for $300.00 and a ribbon," Max said.

"Are you going to buy something for all of us?" Tom asked.

"I bought Bean a new home. I put some money into savings. Later on, I plan to buy a new football and a soccer ball."

"Will you let us use your new balls?" Tom asked.

"I might. You can't put Bean in the teacher's desk, though," Max said.

"I won't do it again," Tom said.

"What about you, Derrick?" Max asked.

"I didn't like getting into trouble, so I won't do it again," Derrick said.

"Let's forget about all that and play," Max said.

"I'm ready," Ken said.

Max and his friends played until Max had to leave. After Max quit playing soccer, he hurried home. Once he entered the kitchen, he asked Mom, "Will you take me to the library?"

"After dinner we can go. Why didn't you ask to go before now?"

"I didn't know what kind of book I wanted then. Now I do. I'm ready to work on my new project."

"You'll have plenty of time to work on it. We'll go if you'd like, though. I might check out some library books."

"I can't wait to get started on my electricity project."

"That's an interesting topic. By the way, who won the most games today?"

"My team won. I guess it's my special day."

"I'm glad you're doing your best in school and on the soccer field."

"It is great to be a winner!" Max shouted.

"You are always a winner when you do your best."

"I know. Receiving a prize makes winning even better, though."

About the Author

Patricia Cruzan is the author of *Sketches of Life*, *Tall Tales of the United States*, and *Molly's Mischievous Dog*. Her books and other writings reflect her experiences in England, France, and Australia. She also has lived or traveled in various states throughout the United States. Patricia lives in Georgia with her husband and dog.

Visit her web site at www.pats-childrens-books.com to find out more about her other books.

ISBN 141206581-X
9781412065818